The text of this book is set in 11-point Caecilia Roman.
The illustrations are watercolor and ink.

Library of Congress Cataloging-in-Publication Data
Evans, Cambria.
Martha moth makes socks / written and illustrated by Cambria Evans.
    p. cm.
Summary: Martha the moth is so hungry while she is fixing dinner for her birthday guests that she eats all the delicious woolies in the house except for a pair of mismatched socks.
  ISBN 0-618-55745-8 (hardcover)
[1. Birthdays—Fiction. 2. Moths—Fiction. 3. Parties—Fiction. 4. Gifts—Fiction.] I. Title.
PZ7.C452867Mar 2006   [E]—dc22   2005003919

ISBN-13: 978-0618-55745-5

Manufactured in China
SCP 10 9 8 7 6 5 4 3 2 1

Martha opened the small door to her pantry.

To her surprise, the only thing inside was dust.

Martha had been so busy planning her birthday
dinner that she had forgotten to buy the food!

So she made a list of ingredients,

buttoned up her coat,

and flew to the store.

Martha could have spent hours choosing between all the tasty treats, but she was in a hurry to start cooking. She quickly purchased the finest polka-dot scarf she had ever smelled, two itchy socks, a shrunken sweater, and two different kinds of yarn. Delicious!

Back home, Martha's stomach growled with hunger.
"While the oven is getting hot, I will just sample this
scarf to make sure it is good," she thought.

It was very tasty, and before she knew it...

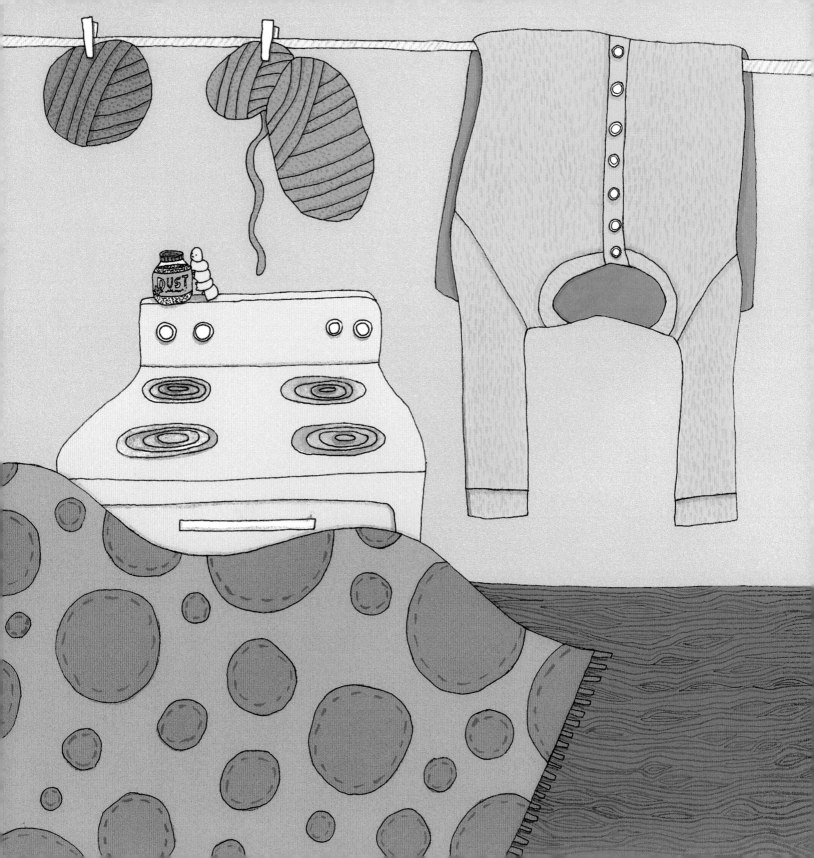

the entire scarf was gone.

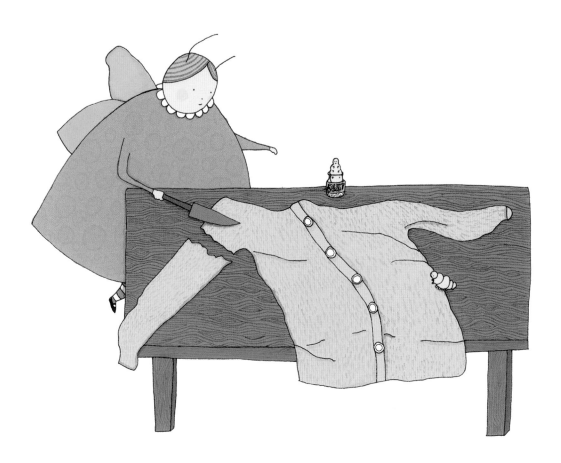

Martha chopped up the sweater, sprinkled it with dust, and thought, "While the water is boiling, I will just taste this sweater to make sure it is also good."

It was even tastier than the scarf, and in no time at all...

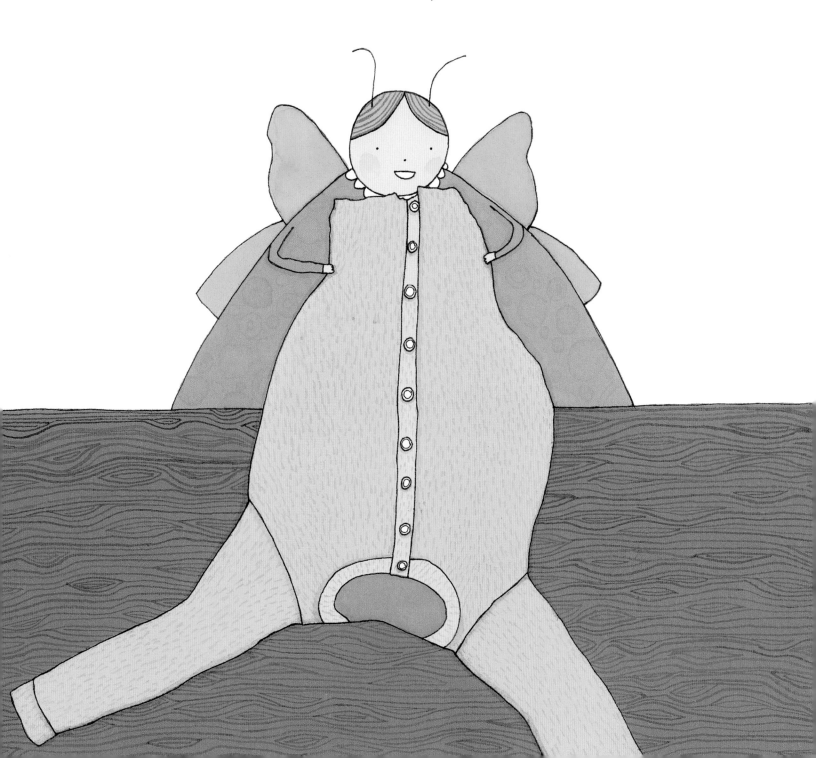

it, too, had disappeared.

Next, Martha heated a saucepan while she mixed the two delightful kinds of yarn together. Martha thought, "While this pan heats up, I will just see if this yarn tastes as good as it looks."

So she twirled the yarn around her fork, slurped it up, and just as before...

it vanished!

Now the only things left to cook were the socks.

But before she could prepare them, the doorbell chimed.
"Is it suppertime already?" Martha said as she fluttered to
the door. Her friends Flit and Flora had arrived. After
birthday greetings, Martha's friends sat down at the table,
which was set with Martha's very best china.

"Dinner smells fabulous!" said Flora.

"Oh, my," Martha said. Had she eaten
everything except a mismatched pair
of itchy wool socks? She blushed.

"Don't worry," said Flit. "Just open your presents."

To her surprise,

the box was filled with dust. "Wonderful!
It is my favorite kind. And I just ran out,"
Martha said.

So together they chopped,

sprinkled,

boiled,

and twirled.

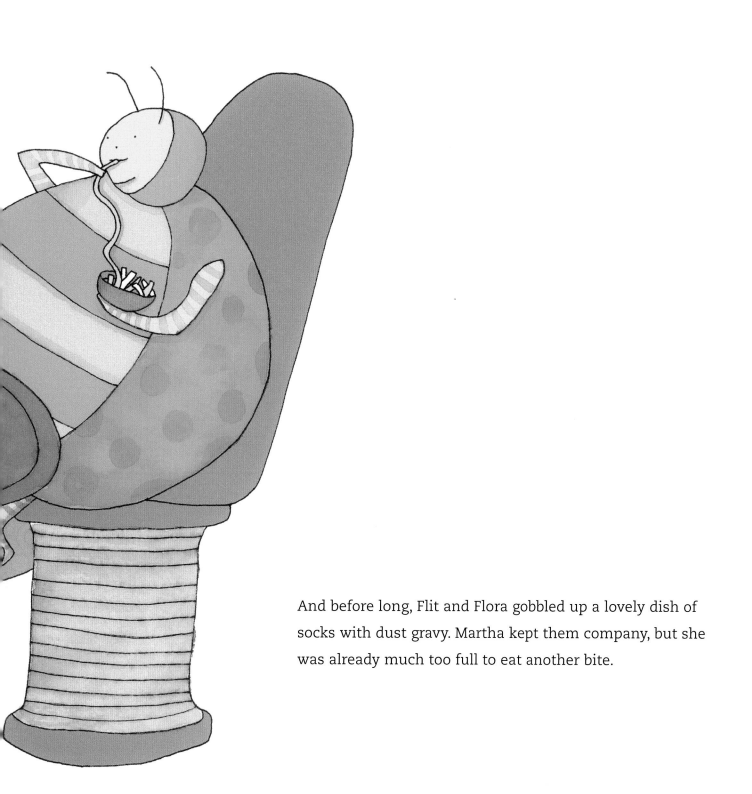

And before long, Flit and Flora gobbled up a lovely dish of socks with dust gravy. Martha kept them company, but she was already much too full to eat another bite.

the end